About the Author

Robert Louis Stevenson was born in Edinburgh, Scotland in 1850. The son of an engineer, Stevenson followed in his father's footsteps by studying engineering and law at the University of Edinburgh. However, his passion for writing soon became more than a hobby, and he decided to pursue it on a full-time basis. This career choice initially upset his father, but Stevenson made a promise to complete his studies, and was admitted to the Scottish Bar in 1875.

Stevenson's most famous work is the classic pirate tale *Treasure Island*, which was published in 1883. A fast-paced story of adventure, with mass appeal, it soon became popular across the world. In the 125 years since then, readers of all ages have delighted in following the exploits of young Jim Hawkins as he travels to a remote island in search of buried gold. Stevenson later created an infamous, but very intriguing, character in *The Strange Case of Dr Jekyll and Mr Hyde*, published in 1886. His adventure story *Kidnapped*, a tale of a young boy and a stolen inheritance, was also published in the same year.

Throughout his life, Stevenson was frequently in poor health, and he often travelled abroad in search of places with mild climates. He also wrote a number of essays detailing these trips. During one such journey to France, he met an American woman named Frances Osbourne, and later married her during a visit to California.

In 1887, Stevenson headed for America with his wife, stepson and mother. He had become famous in New York, and received many attractive offers from various publishers. It was soon after this move that he took up his pen for *The Master of Ballantrae*, a novel which is considered one of his best works.

Stevenson eventually settled, with his family, on the island of Samoa, where he died at the age of forty-four on 3rd December 1894. While best known for writing tales of action and adventure, Robert Louis Stevenson is also remembered as an accomplished poet and essayist.

LONG JOHN SILVER

BILLY BONES

JIM HAWKINS

DR LIVESEY

BEN GUNN

SQUIRE TRELAWNEY

♪ Fifteen men on the dead man's chest —
Yo-ho-ho, and a bottle of rum!

My friends have asked me to write the story of Treasure Island. And I shall hold nothing back, except the location of the island, because treasure is still buried there.

I'll start at the time when my father owned the Admiral Benbow Inn, and an old sailor with a sword came to lodge under our roof.

This is a handy cove and a pleasant place to drink. Yes, it'll do just fine.
How long will you be staying, sir?
I'll stay for a while. You can call me captain.
Sometimes, he would shock our country people with his dreadful stories about hanging, and walking the plank, and storms at sea, and the Dry Tortugas*, and wild deeds and places on the Spanish Main.
The gale nearly rolled our ship twice, and pirates attacked us the next morning!
And sometimes, he would sing his wicked, wild sea songs. I often heard the house shaking with 'yo-ho-ho and a bottle of rum'. Everyone would join in, scared for their lives.
*The Dry Tortugas are a small group of islands in the Gulf of Mexico.
What's your name, lad?
Jim Hawkins. My father owns this inn.
Keep an eye open for a seafaring man with one leg, and I'll pay you for your troubles.
Yes, Captain!
After that, on stormy nights, when the wind shook the house, the man with one leg haunted my dreams.

Not long after this, the first of a series of mysterious events occurred that got rid of the captain. But that did not free us of his affairs.

It was a bitter cold winter, with long, hard frosts and heavy gales.

My mother and I had the inn to ourselves, and we were kept busy, without having to pay much attention to our unpleasant guest.

Oooh!

My poor father's health deteriorated daily, and it was clear that he was unlikely to see the spring.

How is father?

Dr Livesey will be coming to see him again today.

It was very early one January morning when the captain set out down the beach.

My mother was upstairs with my father and, while I was laying the breakfast table...

...and the next instant, I saw Black Dog running away, and the captain chasing after him.

They should have called you Yellow Dog!

Black Dog, in spite of his wound, quickly disappeared over the edge of the hill in no time at all.

Jim! Rum! I must get away from here. I need rum.

Captain, are you hurt?

Just get the rum, laddie.

Uhhh.

Captain!

Dr Livesey and my mother, alarmed by the cries, came running downstairs.

Dear me, what a disgrace upon the house! What shall we do?

You go upstairs to your husband, Mrs Hawkins. I'll do my best to save this fellow's worthless life.

I fetched a basin of water for the doctor. When I returned, he had already ripped the captain's sleeve open, and exposed his great muscular arm.

Where's Black Dog?

There's no Black Dog here.

'Billy Bones' was tattooed on his forearm. And near his shoulder was a man hanging from some gallows.

You have had a stroke. Remember, rum means death for you. Now, Mr Bones--

They're after my old sea chest. Old Flint gave it to me at Savannah when he was dying.

They'll have the black spot* on me soon.

What's that?

*Whenever a piece of paper with a black spot in the middle was given to an accused pirate, it meant that he would be executed.

It's a summons.

The only money I want from you is what you owe my father. Here's one glass, but I'll get you no more.

Can I get a mug of rum for a piece of gold?

Aye! Aye!

21

The book had some scraps of writing in it - the type of thing a lazy man with time on his hands would write.

I can't make head or tail of this. Who is Flint?

He was the bloodthirstiest pirate that ever sailed!

And this is his account book. Now, what else do we have here?

It included dates and amounts and seemingly random words. The record that had been kept lasted for nearly twenty years. At the end of it was a grand total and, following that, the words 'Bones, his pile' appeared.

The paper had been sealed in several places and the squire opened them with great care.

Let's have a look at this. Oh, my goodness!

What? What is it, man? Out with it!

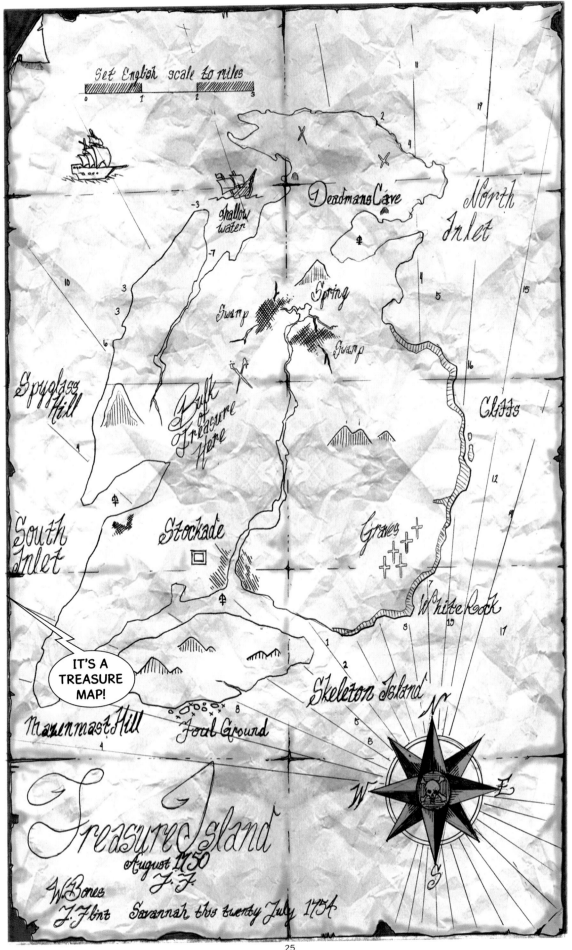

Preparing to go to sea took much longer than the squire had imagined.

Doctor Livesey went to London to find a physician to look after his practice, while the squire was in Bristol getting things ready.

I stayed on at the hall under the supervision of old Tom Redruth, the gamekeeper. I was almost a prisoner...

Dear Livesey,
Our ship is ready. Her name is the Hispaniola. So now, you must not lose an hour and come fast. Jim should also go and see his mother for one night with Redruth for a guard. Then, both of you should come full speed to Bristol.

John Trelawney

...but was full of sea dreams. The weeks passed by, till one day a letter arrived for Dr Livesey. In his absence, I read it.

I was beside myself with glee.

We're off to Bristol, Tom!

Oh, I see.

The next morning, he and I set out on foot for the Admiral Benbow, and there I found my mother in good health.

Promise me you'll be careful!

Dr Livesey and Squire Trelawney will be there too, Mother. Don't worry.

The next day, after dinner, Redruth and I were on the road again. I must have dozed a great deal during the journey. When I woke up, we were standing in front of a large building in a city street. And it was already broad daylight.

Although I had lived by the shore all my life, I had never been near the sea till then. The smell of tar and salt was something new, and I saw some of the most wonderful figureheads.

I saw many old sailors, with rings in their ears, and whiskers curled in ringlets, and pigtails, and their swaggering, clumsy sea-walk. I could not have been more delighted if I had seen as many kings or archbishops.

Long John Silver was to be the ship's cook. And it was he, along with the squire, that had got the crew together. They were tough fellows, of unconquerable spirit.

The *Hispaniola* lay some way out. At last, however, we stepped aboard...

Welcome aboard, men!

...and were greeted by the mate, Mr Arrow, a brown old sailor.

What do you wish to discuss, Captain Smollett? All well, I hope. All shipshape and seaworthy?

Well, sir, I had better speak straight. I don't like this cruise. I don't like the men and I don't like my officer. There, that's short and sweet.

Before we had even set sail, the captain asked to meet with Squire Trelawney.

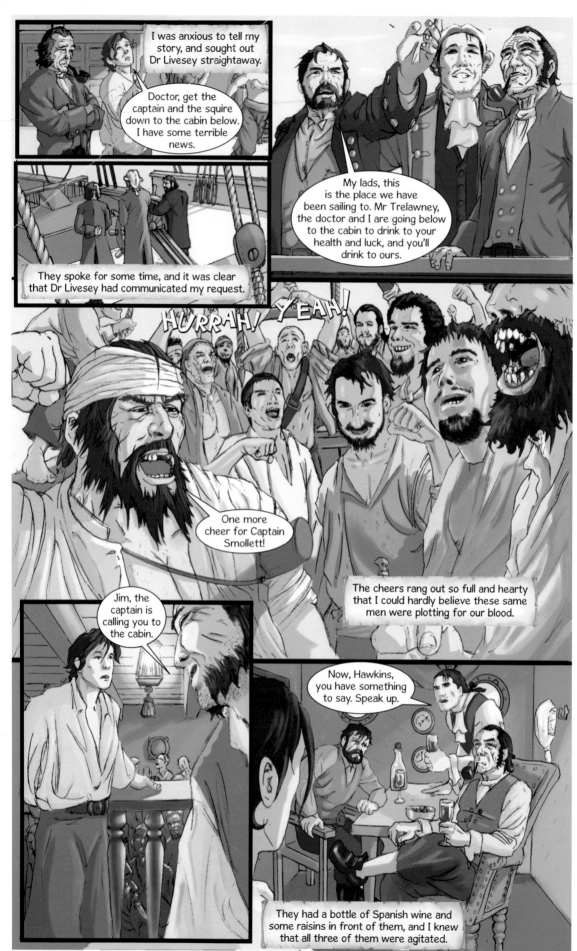

The appearance of the island, when I came on deck the next morning, was completely different. We were now lying just to the south-east of the low eastern coast.

Although there was hardly any breeze, we had covered a great deal of distance during the night.

Woods covered a large part of the surface and the general colouring was uniform and sad.

Perhaps it was because of the way the island looked — with its melancholy trees, and wild stone spires, and with the surf foaming and thundering on the beach — that I hated the very thought of Treasure Island.

You would have thought anyone would have been glad to get to land after being at sea for so long. Yet, my heart sank into my boots at the first sight of this island.

They're aiming for the flag. Would it not be wiser to take it down?

Strike my colours? No, sir, not I!

The aim of the second shot was better, but the ball knocked down a tree, doing no further damage.

CRASH

It's low tide now. Let's see if we can recover any supplies from the water.

Hello, Jim!

Dr Livesey. Captain!

I had reached the stockade safe and sound.

We thought we'd lost you, Jim!

No, sir!

Good — we now have more eyes for guard duty.

Tom was buried before supper, as we didn't know when the pirates would return.

I'm going to miss Tom.

You'll never find the treasure. And you won't be able to sail away. There's not a man among you fit to sail the ship.

You're making a big mistake!

And with a dreadful oath, Silver stumbled off.

My lads, we're outnumbered. I don't need to tell you that. But we have the advantage of fighting from shelter. I am sure we can defeat them.

Captain Smollett then told us his plan for defence.

Each of us stood guard at our posts.

Hang them! This is as dull as the doldrums.

KRACK

Here they come!

To your stations!

POW

How many on your side, Livesey?

Three shots were fired from this side, Captain.

And how many on yours, Squire Trelawney?

An hour passed, with no sign of the pirates. But then...

...several bullets struck the log house, but not one entered.

The scheme I had in my head wasn't a bad one.

First, I went to find Ben Gunn's coracle.

Then, I slipped out under the cover of night, and made my way towards the *Hispaniola*.

Soon I reached the ship's hawser. My plan was to cut her adrift and let her go ashore where she pleased.

The hawser was as stiff as a bowstring. And the current was so strong, that the ship pulled upon her anchor.

SNIKK

With my knife, I cut one strand after another...

...till the vessel was nearly free.

Uhh!

SNAP

I waited for the breeze to come again and, when the hawser became loose, I cut the last fibres.

I then began to hear the sound of loud voices from the cabin.

CRASH

SMACK

Through the window I saw two men arguing fiercely. One of them was Israel Hands.

I can't really say why I took hold of that cord. I suppose curiosity got the better of me.

Both men were not only drunk, but also furiously angry.

You drunk fool!

ARGH!

My scheme complete, I set off for the shore in my coracle.

The joke's on you now, Silver!

Alas, the current began to carry me away. I heard noises from the ship and knew that the pirates had been awakened to a sense of disaster.

Scared of being caught, I lay low in the skiff for hours.

Gradually my weariness grew, until sleep overcame me.

It was broad daylight when I woke up and found myself at the south-west end of Treasure Island.

The current was still too strong for me to control my coracle and I was not able to land on the rocks.

I don't like the idea of trying to land on these rocks and having to face these fearsome looking creatures. I'll try to paddle round to a safer part of the island.

The current carried me to the next reach of open sea, and there in front of me was the *Hispaniola*.

It was clear that nobody was steering the ship.

I managed to bring myself up close to the *Hispaniola*.

Either they were drunk or had deserted her.

If I can paddle up to the ship, I could easily take control of her.

As I climbed, a dull blow told me that the *Hispaniola* had struck my coracle. I was left without retreat.

You give me food and drink and I'll tell you how to sail her.

Okay, let's head for the north inlet and put her ashore there.

We struck our bargain on the spot.

In three minutes, I had the *Hispaniola* sailing easily along the coast of Treasure Island.

I was very happy with my new command, and pleased with the bright, sunny weather and the prospects of the coast.

Tell me, Jim, do you think a dead man is as good as dead, or does he come alive again?

You can kill the body but not the spirit, Mr Hands. O'Brien there is in another world, and may still be watching us.

Well, that's unfortunate. Looks like killing him was a waste of time.

Jim, can you bring me a bottle of wine? This brandy is too strong for my head.

Some wine? White or red?

Any, as long as it's strong and there's plenty of it.

All right, I'll bring you port wine, Mr Hands. But I'll have to look for it.

I didn't believe the idea of him preferring wine to brandy. The whole story was an excuse. He wanted me to leave the deck.

I quietly returned to spy on my companion.

Where's my knife?

Then, suddenly...

Uhh!

BLAM

...he pinned me to the mast by my shoulder. And in the surprise of the moment, both my pistols went off.

SPLASH

My wound pained me a good deal and bled freely, but it was neither deep nor dangerous.

Hngh!

I dropped both my pistols and they fell into the water along with Israel Hands.

Leaving the *Hispaniola* by the bay, I moved away from the sea.

I was anxious to get home to the stockade and boast of my achievements.

There was no doubt they kept a bad watch.

PECK

ZZZZZZZ

PECK
PECK

If it had been Silver and his lads who were now creeping in on them, not one of them would have seen daybreak.

It was completely dark. However, I could hear the steady drone of the snorers and a small occasional noise – a flickering or pecking that I could not understand.

After digging for several hours...

Well, blow me down!

The seven hundred thousand pounds, all gone.

...it was very clear; the treasure had been found and taken away.

Each of the men was shocked. But with Silver the blow passed almost instantly.

Every thought of his soul had been set on that money. But he kept his head and his temper, and adjusted his plan before the others had had time to realise their disappointment.

The pirates, with oaths and cries, began to leap, one after another, into the pit, and to dig with their fingers.

Ben Gunn was on deck alone.

I helped him escape only to save your lives. Silver is too dangerous a man to have on board.

But this was not all. Silver had not gone empty-handed.

♪ ♫ Fifteen men on the dead man's chest... ♪

He had taken one of the sacks of coins, worth perhaps three or four hundred guineas, to help him on his way.

I think we were all pleased to be rid of him so easily.

To cut a long story short, we then got a few hands on board and cruised back home.

Mr Gray not only saved his money but, with his desire to rise, also studied his profession. He is now mate, and part owner, of a fine fully-equipped ship, besides being married and having children.

We all received a good share of the treasure and used it wisely or foolishly according to our nature.

Ben Gunn received a thousand pounds, which he lost in three weeks or, to be exact, nineteen days. He was back begging on the twentieth day.

83

Captain Smollett decided to retire from the sea.

Of Silver, we heard no more.

That formidable seafaring man with one leg has, at last, gone out of my life.

Perhaps he will pay for his misdeeds in the future.

We weren't able to bring all the treasure back, and some of it still lies where Flint buried it. But it can stay there.

Nothing will take me back to that accursed island. The worst dreams I ever have are of the surf booming about its coasts, and I often start upright in bed with the sharp voice of Captain Flint still ringing in my ears...

Pieces of eight! Pieces of eight!

ABOUT US

It is night-time in the forest. A campfire is crackling, and the storytelling has begun. In the warm, cheerful radiance of the campfire, the storyteller's audience is captivated.

Inspired by this enduring relationship between a campfire and gripping storytelling, we bring you four series of Campfire Graphic Novels:

Our Classics adapt timeless literature from some of the greatest writers ever.

Our Mythology series features epics, myths, and legends from around the world – tales that transport readers to lands of mystery and magic.

Our Biography titles bring to life remarkable and inspiring figures from history.

Our Originals line showcases exciting new characters and stories from some of today's most talented graphic novelists and illustrators.

We hope you will gather round our campfire and discover the fascinating stories and characters inside our books.

CAMPFIRE™

PIRATES AHOY!

The Golden Age of Piracy was approximately the period between the mid-17th and mid-18th centuries.

BLACKBEARD

Edward Teach, better known as the fearsome **Blackbeard** because of his long facial hair, was an infamous English pirate in the early 18th century. His reign of terror lasted two long years (1716-18), during which time he plundered many merchant ships on the Caribbean Sea and the Atlantic Ocean. He was always well-armed with several pistols, knives, and a sword aboard his ship – *Queen Anne's Revenge*. And can you guess what he did to scare his enemies? He lit matches under his hat or braided them into his beard to make it appear that his head was on fire. The crew of many ships surrendered at the mere sight of this frightful man. He was eventually killed in a battle with government forces in 1718.

DID YOU KNOW?

The **Jolly Roger** was the name given to the flag hoisted by pirates on their ships. It usually had a skull above two long bones which were set in an x pattern on a piece of black cloth. It was meant to strike fear into the hearts of victims!

THE PIRATES' CODE OF CONDUCT

Surprising but true: pirates followed their own set of strict rules. The codes varied from ship to ship, but had a common aim – to keep the crew from doing anything wrong. Some general codes included:

- All the members of the crew would get a fair share of the booty.
- A deserter or anyone keeping any secret from the rest would be marooned on an island, or in a small boat, with just some gunpowder, a bottle of water, and a gun with one bullet.
- A lazy man, or one who failed to keep his weapons clean, would lose his share of the booty.
- Every member would get a share of any captured drink and fresh food.
- Gambling was forbidden.
- Every member was compensated for the loss of a leg or hand in battle.

CAPTAIN KIDD

A British pirate, **William Kidd**, became known as one of the most infamous outlaws of all time. He plundered ships along the coast of North America, the Caribbean and the Indian Ocean in the 17th century, and accumulated a great deal of wealth. It is believed that **Captain Kidd** buried treasure from the plundered ship, *Quedagh Merchant*, on Gardiner's Island in the USA, before he was executed in 1701. Though some of it was found, legend has it that a large quantity still remains undiscovered. Over the years, many people have searched for it in vain. Treasure hunters have even gone down to the depths of the ocean in the hope of discovering the notorious pirate's great treasure.

DID YOU KNOW?

Pirates often fell sick because of the lack of good food. Scurvy, a disease caused by the lack of vitamin C, was a common ailment. Pirates knew they had it when their teeth started falling out and their skin began to go pale!

PIRATE SHIPS

Contrary to popular depictions, pirates generally used small and speedy ships rather than huge galleons. Two of the most popular ships in the Golden Age of Piracy were sloops and schooners:

SLOOPS

Light and manoeuvrable, **sloops** had shallow draughts which helped them sail into shallow waters to escape from, or chase, other ships. They could sail quickly, even without any wind, and with just a few pairs of oars. They were relatively small and usually contained up to 75 men and 14 guns.

SCHOONERS

Fast-moving ships, **schooners** had narrow hulls that allowed them to navigate easily over shoals and shallow waters. They had the capacity to take a full load and the 75-man crew inland, to hide in caves or to divide the pirates' spoils. Captain Smollett's ship, *Hispaniola*, is a schooner.